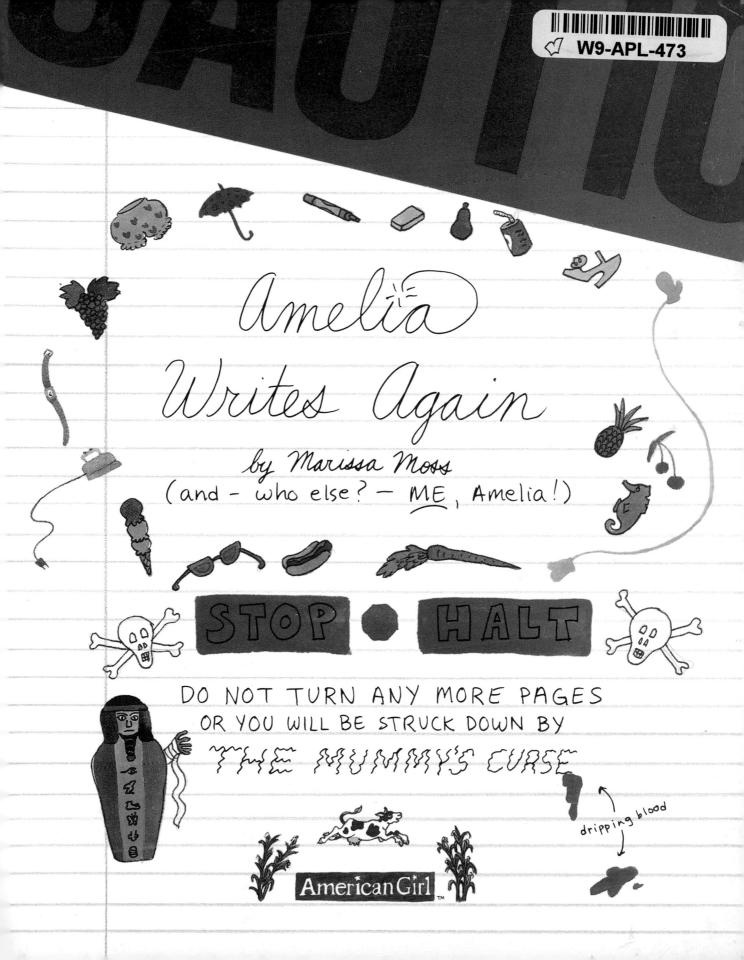

Amelia Writes Again

by Marissa Moss
(and - who else? - ME, Amelia!)

STOP • HALT

DO NOT TURN ANY MORE PAGES
OR YOU WILL BE STRUCK DOWN BY
THE MUMMY'S CURSE

dripping blood

American Girl™

This is NOT a spelling mistake— it's her name!

This notebook is dedicated to
→ Liisa,
because she liked the first one so much,
and to Journal Writers Everywhere.

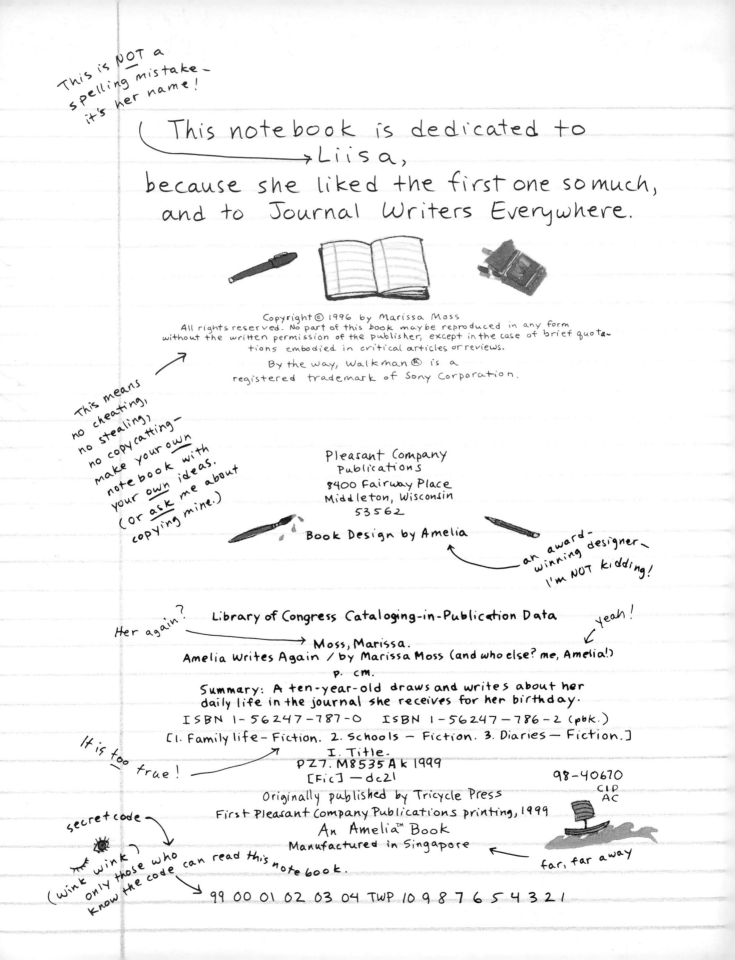

This means no cheating, no stealing, no copycatting— make your own notebook with your own ideas. (or ask me about copying mine.)

Pleasant Company Publications
8400 Fairway Place
Middleton, Wisconsin
53562

Book Design by Amelia

an award-winning designer— I'm NOT kidding!

Her again?

Library of Congress Cataloging-in-Publication Data

Yeah!

Moss, Marissa.
Amelia Writes Again / by Marissa Moss (and who else? me, Amelia!)
p. cm.
Summary: A ten-year-old draws and writes about her daily life in the journal she receives for her birthday.
ISBN 1-56247-787-0   ISBN 1-56247-786-2 (pbk.)
[1. Family life—Fiction. 2. Schools—Fiction. 3. Diaries—Fiction.]
I. Title.
PZ7.M8535 Ak 1999
[Fic]—dc21
98-40670
CIP
AC

It is too true!

Originally published by Tricycle Press
First Pleasant Company Publications printing, 1999
An Amelia™ Book
Manufactured in Singapore

far, far away

secret code
(wink wink)
only those who know the code can read this notebook.

99 00 01 02 03 04 TWP 10 9 8 7 6 5 4 3 2 1

This is my beautiful, new, **BLANK** notebook, waiting for me to fill it with words and drawings. But I feel as blank and empty as these pages. I mean, I just turned **10** exciting years old, but I feel exactly the same as when I was 9. And I look the same,

same brain, same ideas, same thoughts

me

same old scar from when Cleo threw a toy teapot at me — that's my stupid sister's idea of a tea party!

ears are still not pierced (not till I'm 16, says mom)

same dip under my nose — what is this thing called anyway, and what's it for?

I still had a good birthday, but I expected **SOMETHING** would change. I thought ten was close to teen — almost a teenager. It's not.

Miss Know-It-All Cleo. If she knows so much, how come she can't eat pizza without getting it all over her face? I call her Cheezy chin.

piece o' pizza

gooey, gluey cheese

gooey, gluey chin

Cleo says no matter how old I am, I'll always be a jerky little sister. And she'll always get to do things first. But she's wrong.

souvenir stamped penny from Space World

lunar surface- *not* swiss cheese

I got to go to Space World <u>first</u>, for my birthday. Just me, Mom, and Leah. The best part was the Lunar Landing Ride. When Cleo asked what it was like, I said she'd have to find out for herself, <u>if</u> she ever gets to go.

ticket stub from Space World

postcard from Gift Shop

Special sensitized magnetic strip that sets off Cleo-alarm if she touches any part of this notebook

I bought this postcard just to put in my new notebook. But when I did, Leah asked if she could see what I write in here. I said maybe. She may be my new best friend, but I don't know if I want her to see my private thoughts and drawings. What if she laughs at me or thinks I'm dumb?

One thing is sure, I <u>NEVER</u> want Cleo to see what's in here.

my new paintset

my new brush

Anyway, guess who gave me this notebook for my birthday? Not Nadia. She sent me a beautiful watercolor set with a great brush. Not Leah. She gave me a charm bracelet to match her own. Not even Mom. She gave me a Walkman.

ribbon from Nadia's present— she's still my best friend, even far away, but Leah's my best friend, too, now. Can you have 2 best friends? Isn't one always best-est? I know Nadia better, but Leah's here, which is definitely better, except when she asks to read my notebook

← spilled grape juice — NOT! it's purple paint from my new paint set

birthday card from Nadia — she drew it herself

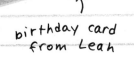
birthday card from Leah

It was Cleo!!! She said now I could write something NICE about her for a change.

But you hafta write good stuff about me.

Thanks!

She didn't say EVERYTHING I wrote about her had to be nice. Just something.

Here goes: Cleo does have 1 good thing about her — her hands. She has long, elegant fingers and she doesn't chew on her fingernails the way I do.

Some hands have short, stubby fingers. I call them Glove Hands.

← fingerprint

plate of spaghetti

← hairy bug

↑ furball

← witch hand or claw

Glove Hand ↑

Some hands are all bony.

you can count on a limp handshake with _this_ hand →

← droopy, drippy hand

hand with pinchy fingers — I call these Twig Hands →

fingers going sight- seeing — oh, no! I drew 6 fingers! what a sight to see!

Some hands seem smart. Others seem dumb. And this has nothing to do with whether the people they belong to are stupid or smart. It's just the way the hands look. Wide-awake or droopy, itchy or snooty, pinchy or thick.

← fingers going for a walk

fingers meaning business →

I like to watch deaf people's hands. It's like watching expressions fly across someone's face or hearing feelings.

bunny fingers hopping around

duck fingers making shadows on a wall

There's a kid in my class, Eli. He has _great_ hands, but better than that, he has the most amazing gestures. It's like his hands are having their own conversation while he's talking.

It's hard to show movement in a still drawing, but it's kind of like this

Don't interrupt me!

I'm not!

I keep trying to start my math homework, but I always get distracted by my hand that's doing the writing, and then I get distracted by the numbers.

Numbers each have their own personalities.

It's hard to be an odd number!

5 is sharp and cranky.

I'm even-tempered.

4 is friendly and patient.

3 is jolly but lazy and never wants to budge.

I'm too full to budge. I'll just stay here.

It's tough being #1.

1 is stand-offish, probably because she's first.

different stamps have different numbers on them

stamps from letters from Nadia— she's great at math. I wish she could help me.

32 CELEBRATING WILDLIFE
HIP HIP HOORAY

Before I know it, I'm telling myself a story about the numbers in the problem.

Like 5 is all mad at 2

for being a copycat (only upside down and backwards, which is even worse as far as 5 is concerned), so the 2 of them are hissing at each other when they're supposed to stand together and be divided by 6 ½.

But 6 is too busy taking care of baby

½ ← stinky diapoo

who needs his diaper changed, to pay any attention to

You think you're so smart! I'm more than you! I count more!

5 2

Yeah? Well, more isn't always better. You can be more of a jerk, so there!

Then Mom says it's dinnertime, and

numbers refusing to cooperate and running away, leaving me with a big, fat

Hmmm... take a left at Venus, right at Mars, straight past Pluto, and where are you.?

My paper is still blank. That is, there are no answers written down, although there are lots of doodles in the margins. Last night's homework ended up looking like a map made by an alien instead of a math worksheet.

Sometimes this happens during a quiz, which is really bad. I end up handing in a no-answer quiz.

me, sinking into the floor

blank quiz

Mr. Nudel's big teacher desk

scribbled math worksheet

Mr. Nudel says I just have to concentrate, he knows I can do it. I know I can do it, too, so if we both know I can do it, why do I actually have to do it?

Now, Amelia, use that old noodle.

in cartoons, men don't have eyelashes — in real life, they do marshmallows sticking to the roof of the page

confused ant — which marshmallow is real?

Mut-ant — too many
legs caused by eating
too many marshmallows

the ants go marching one by one looking for a marshmallow crumb

I started to write a good thing about Cleo, which is hard. But I do remember a fun game Cleo and I used to play when we were little. It works like this:

Take a package of big FLUFFY marshmallows — not the mini, the BIG kind. Then you squash one in your fingers till it gets all sticky. Next

THROW it on the ceiling.
It should stick!
See whose sticks the
longest. Try to catch
it in your mouth when
it falls. (It will fall. They
don't stick forever.)

marshmallow falling into the gaping mouth

actual marshmallow

this is not
a purple
marshmallow —
it's shadow

drawing of marshmallows

PUFFY
FLUFFS

guess whose
gaping mouth this is —
the jelly roll nose
is a clue

Once, we were way too noisy, and Mom walked into the room. Luckily, the marshmallows were all stuck to the ceiling and she didn't look up and see them. (who looks at ceilings anyway? NO ONE!)

ceiling

marshmallows

about to drop—oh, no!

what's all this noise about? what's going on here?

Nothing.

Nothing.

marshmallow in cheek — making a lump — I hope Mom doesn't notice

sorry, Mom, I didn't mean to make you fat

Sometimes Cleo CAN be fun, but not often — I think the marshmallows were her idea

bag of marshmallows behind Cleo's back

Just as she left, they started to drop! We were sure lucky none fell on her head.

sticky marshmallow

hairy marshmallow

imagine washing marshmallow out of your hair—yuucch!

chopsticks are no easier for me at 10 than at 9 — does anything change?

↓

rice falling / time to use a fork ↑

last night I got this fortune in my fortune cookie — too true!

A friendship is testing you.

I told Leah about the marshmallow game. I thought she would laugh, but she's still mad at me.

"When are you going to show me your notebook?" she's always asking now. "What's the big deal? Am I your friend or not?"

She is my friend. Part of me wants to show it to her. But part of me doesn't.

It's my notebook!

Help!

No! It's my notebook!

amelia write again!

↑ me fighting myself over whether or not I should show this to Leah

Today was really terrible. Leah wouldn't even eat lunch with me. She said if I can't be honest with her, I'm not much of a friend. Is keeping some things private the same as being dishonest?

my lonely lunch →

wilted lettuce and cheese sandwich ↓

bruised apple ↓

crumbled cookies ↓

↑ nothing tasted good →

I thought yesterday was bad, but now a HORRIBLE, AWFUL thing has happened.

Much, much worse than any fight with Leah.

There was a big fire at our school last night, and the fire department says it was arson. That means someone set it ON PURPOSE!!

I heard a lot of sirens, but I didn't know it was my school till I got there this morning.

← piece of charred wood, probably from a desk

There was a crowd of reporters and yellow CAUTION tape across one whole wing of the school. That wing was all black and crumbly like slices of burnt this was very hard to draw — a mess just looks like a mess

CAUTION CAUTION CAUTION CAUTION CAUTION CAUTION CAUTION CAUTION CAUTIO

toast with bites taken out, and it smelled smoky like the time Mom left a potholder on the stove by mistake.

mr. Nudel

Leah

Max

Mrs. Kravitz, the music teacher

Mom's burnt potholder

First thing, instead of the Pledge of Allegiance or anything, we were all herded into the cafeteria, and Ms. Bell, the principal, told us that somebody had set fire to our school, but no one was hurt, and the creep who did it was somebody

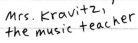

she didn't say CREEP exactly — she said arsonist. that means CREEP!!

Ms. Bell — her fingers held the podium tight, tight

protesting something, but we're not sure what, and we're not to worry.

And it will take a long time to rebuild, and portables will be set up next week.

portable classrooms rushing to us, even this minute

Then we went on a tour of the burned part so we could all see what it looked like. What it looked like was terrible! Burnt books, papers, parts of desks and bulletin boards.

The burned part was the first and second grades. Not my classroom. I'm really glad about that, at least. But I feel kind of bad about feeling glad. I can't help it, I a_m glad. Is that bad?

bits of broken glass everywhere

regular classroom, like mine

blackboard

door   windows

calendar

bulletin boards with papers on them

bookshelf with books

teacher chair

trash can   big teacher desk

lots of student desks (but I can only fit 4)

burnt-down classroom

burnt door   broken windows

burnt papers

burnt calendar — who knows what day it is?

melted bulletin board

charred bookshelf

burnt-up trash

dented trash can   charred desk

Student desks, fallen all over, with burnt backs, seats, and tables

rubble of books

smoky, smeary mess everywhere — you can barely even see the floor

someone's paper — I hope they didn't work too hard on it

metal and wood pole for opening high windows and shutting them

charcoaled yardstick — now you could write with it

The worst part was Ms. Rooney's classroom. She had brought her own comfy armchair to school, her own books, her own light-up globe. All that stuff was ruined.

black patches all over

springs springing out

torn-up bits

I saw her sitting in her blackened chair with the sunflowers on it. She was crying, but not making a sound. It made me feel awful to see her.

I wrote Nadia a long letter about the fire, and I'm writing about it here in my notebook, too, but I still can't get it out of my head.

Sometimes getting things outside of me and onto paper helps. Not this time. I keep seeing Ms. Rooney with the tears running down her cheeks.

trying to mail my troubles away

To: Nadia

Leah

me

At least Leah's not mad at me anymore. Or maybe she's forgotten about my notebook. No one can think of anything but the fire.

Even Cleo has been nice.

me watching T.V. on the nubby green rug

Cleo bringing me cinnamon toast and hot chocolate

But the yellow tape is still up. I won't feel better until it's gone.

jack

ducky barrette

bus token

die (it's not dead—it's one dice)

Yesterday the workers started to rebuild the school, and I got a great idea. I told Mr. Nudel, and he told Ms. Bell, and she thinks my idea is great, too!

↑ rubber ball

They said

button

So this is what we get to do:

When the workers pour new cement for a new pavement in front of the new classrooms, each kid is supposed to bring a treasure from home, like a plastic dinosaur, a button, a seashell — anything!

tiny plastic clothespin

little toy baby bottle

And we each get to put our treasure in the wet cement and write our initials next to it.

heart bead

metal car

wind-up chattering teeth

broken geode

plastic dinosaur

rubbery snake

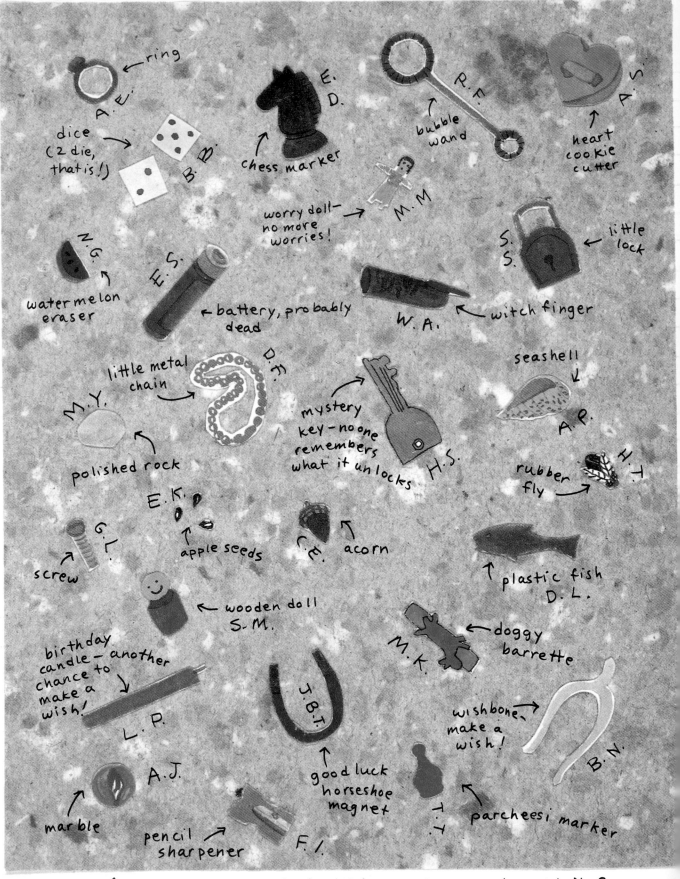

- ring — A.E.
- dice (2 die, that is!) — B.B.
- chess marker — E.D.
- bubble wand — R.F.
- heart cookie cutter — A.S.
- worry doll — no more worries! — M.M
- little lock — S.S.
- watermelon eraser — N.G.
- battery, probably dead — E.S.
- witch finger — W.A.
- little metal chain — D.F.
- mystery key — no one remembers what it unlocks — H.S.
- seashell — A.P.
- polished rock — M.Y.
- rubber fly — H.T.
- apple seeds — E.K.
- acorn — C.E.
- screw — G.L.
- plastic fish — D.L.
- wooden doll — S.M.
- doggy barrette — M.K.
- birthday candle — another chance to make a wish! — L.P.
- good luck horseshoe magnet — J.B.T.
- wishbone — make a wish! — B.N.
- marble — A.J.
- pencil sharpener — F.I.
- parcheesi marker — T.T.

< cool paper that looks like cement — mom bought it for me

← checker

iron marker from monopoly game →

my marker, making a different kind of mark!

It was great! I put in a marker because I like to draw and write so much. (It was out of ink, anyway.) Leah put in a charm from her charm bracelet. One first-grader put in a tooth he'd just lost. (He said he still got money from the tooth fairy for it.)

The last person to put something in was Ms. Rooney. She put in her good-luck penny to bring the school and all of us good luck.

Mrs. Kravitz, the music teacher, put in a finger cymbal

Leah's charm, an angel riding a dove

tiny tooth

Ms. Jenko, the P.E. teacher, put in her whistle

Ms. Bell put in a jingle bell

shiny, good-luck penny

Mr. Nudel put in a dry noodle

And for the first time since the fire, I saw Ms. Rooney smile.

no more tears!

same old wrinkles

smile wrinkles

brand-new smile

Ms. Rooney's new cheery chair with cherries on it

I wrote Nadia about my idea, and I drew her a great picture of our new sidewalk. She wrote me back right away.

Nadia's letter—actually, it's a postcard

Lake Cowabunga

Dear Amelia,
I got your great letter and drawing. I sure wish I could put a treasure in the cement, too. I'd put in a bead from my necklace that matches your necklace. I'd put it right next to your marker. I can't wait to visit and see how everything looks. Maybe for winter vacation, Mom says. Your friend forever,
♡♡♡♡ Nadia ♡♡♡♡

27¢ say cheese
In praise of cheese

2¢ LANCELOT

Amelia,
my best friend
564 North Homerest
Oopa, Oregon
97881

this is Nadia the way I remember her — it's been a few months since I moved away, but I still miss her →

I guess I'll always miss her

some stamps sure have strange pictures on them

Things are beginning to feel normal again at school. And they caught the arsonist. (CREEEEP!!) It was some man who wanted to protest against our government. I can't figure out how burning down our school sends a message to the government. Couldn't he just send a letter? Or if he was really in a hurry, a fax?

bushy president eyebrows

baggy president eyes

the President
the White House
Washington, D.C.

letter to the president, like Mom always writes when she doesn't like a law or something—she writes tons of letters, to Congress, to the president, to anyone she thinks should listen

PRIVATE!! for presidential eyes only—official U.S. Business!

I'm so happy everything is all taken care of — the arsonist (still a CREEPULAR CREEPACIOUS CREEP!) and the school.

Now I don't have to worry anymore. Now I can think about writing stories again. If I can think of any. Maybe when I have a story (if it's a good one), I can show my notebook to Leah.

I have an 💡 already!

A Good Luck Story

A girl found a shiny new penny on the sidewalk. She picked it up for good luck and named it Patty so she could call it Pretty Patty Penny (or P.P.P. for short). She put Patty in her pocket, but she didn't know her pocket had a hole in it. The penny fell out, and with it went all of her good luck.

Bad things started to happen to the girl. She dropped her books in a puddle. She punched the tetherball and it hit her

hole in pocket

girl whistling because she feels so lucky

school book

lunch box

"Ouch!" said Pretty Patty Penny. "Being bonked **on** the head is not lucky for me!"

on the head. (ouch!) She sat on her chocolate donut at lunchtime.

Pretty Patty Penny wasn't having much luck either. A seagull tried to eat her but spit her out. A dog lifted its leg over her, but she rolled away just in time. Then a lady in pointy high heels stepped on her. Could things get worse?

P.P.P. needed the girl to find her and pick her up. The girl needed P.P.P. and her good luck. Would they ever find each other again?

On the way home from school, the girl's shoelace came untied. "More bad luck," she thought. But when she bent down to tie it, what did she see? A penny! Not just any penny, but Pretty Patty Penny! This time she put Patty in her <u>other</u> pocket, with no hole in it. She ran all the way home and put Patty in her piggybank. She never had bad luck again, and neither did Pretty Patty Penny.

Leah just passed me a note. It says:

> What are you writing about?
> When can I see your
> notebook? I'll show you
> mine.
>
> (P.S. Mine is full of secrets.)

I just don't know if I should show her. It's hard to decide. Some things should just be for yourself, but some are okay to share with your best friend. Some things are even better when you share them, like Space World. Maybe I should just show her already. Especially if she shows me hers.

Some things just go together, like:

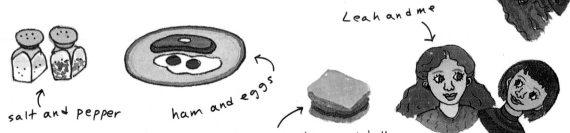

salt and pepper

ham and eggs

peanut butter and jelly

Leah and me

Nadia and me

I have an idea! When I was 9, I only wrote stories by myself. Now I'm 🔟 ⓪, so it's time for a change— I'll write a story <u>WITH</u> Leah IN MY NOTEBOOK!

bad drawing of pointing hand — I know Leah can draw it better

Leah—you can see what's in my notebook by writing in it yourself. Let's do a story together. Here!

Amelia—Great idea! Here's 😊😊 *the first sentence of our story.*

There once was a boy named Nick who had a terrible secret!

He wrote about his secret in his notebook!

His best friend, ~~George~~, begged and begged to read the ~~notebook~~.

please! please! please!

Please! Please! Please!

Finally, Nick said, "Okay. Here." But he was afraid of what George would think of his secret.

George was glad that Nick trusted him with his secret. He → didn't think it was terrible at all!

Nick felt better having someone else know his secret and still like him.

The secret was

that Nick had a tail!

And that's the end

useful for picking things up and carrying them

of this tale!

I like the story Leah and I wrote together. So does she. And now she knows the kind of things I write in here. Maybe I'll show her the rest someday. I guess she felt left out when I wouldn't show her anything. I didn't mean to leave her out. She is my best friend, after all.

But I still worry that if she read what I wrote about numbers and hands, she might think I'm ~~weird~~ ~~wierd~~ ~~weird~~ ~~wierd~~ weird.

I wonder what Leah thinks about and what she writes in her notebook.

Leah thinking about all the good stuff in her own notebook

Now I'm sure that things are okay between us because when Leah saw me staring at her, she asked, "What are you staring at? Do I have something on my face?"

"Yes," I said, and she started wiping her nose and mouth. "Yes!" I said. "Your nose! Your nose is on your face!" And I showed her the picture I drew of her. She laughed! She's a good friend, alright. Maybe I'll show her my <u>next</u> notebook.

BEEP! BEEP! LAST PAGE ALERT — TIME FOR A NEW NOTEBOOK! OH, CLEEEE — OO!

BEEEEEP